MODULI
UNDECIM FESTORUM

RECENT RESEARCHES IN THE MUSIC OF THE RENAISSANCE

James Haar and Howard Mayer Brown, general editors

A-R Editions, Inc., publishes six quarterly series—

Recent Researches in the Music of the Middle Ages and Early Renaissance,
Margaret Bent, general editor;

Recent Researches in the Music of the Renaissance,
James Haar and Howard Mayer Brown, general editors;

Recent Researches in the Music of the Baroque Era,
Robert L. Marshall, general editor;

Recent Researches in the Music of the Classical Era,
Eugene K. Wolf, general editor;

Recent Researches in the Music of the Nineteenth and Early Twentieth Centuries,
Rufus Hallmark, general editor;

Recent Researches in American Music,
H. Wiley Hitchcock, general editor—

which make public music that is being brought to light
in the course of current musicological research.

Each volume in the *Recent Researches* is devoted
to works by a single composer or to a single genre of composition,
chosen because of its potential interest to scholars and performers,
and prepared for publication according to the standards that govern
the making of all reliable historical editions.

Correspondence should be addressed:

A-R EDITIONS, INC.
315 West Gorham Street
Madison, Wisconsin 53703

RECENT RESEARCHES IN THE MUSIC OF THE RENAISSANCE • VOLUME LVI

MODULI
UNDECIM FESTORUM

Edited by J. Heywood Alexander

A-R EDITIONS, INC. • MADISON

Library of Congress Cataloging in Publication Data:

Moduli undecim festorum
    (Recent researches in the music of the Renaissance,
ISSN 0486–123X ; v. 56)
    Motets for 4–5 voices, with or without instruments.
    "Texts and translations": p.
    Edited from the 1st ed. parts (Paris : N. du Chemin,
1554) in the Bayerische Staatsbibliothek, Munich.
    Includes bibiliographical references.
    Contents: Victimae paschali laudes / Jean Maillard —
Ascendo ad patrem / Jean Maillard — Si quis diligit
me / Villefond — [etc.]
    1. Motets.   I. Alexander, J. Heywood.   III. Series.
M2.R2384   vol. 56   [M2082]   83–11926
ISBN 0–89579–186–2

Contents

Preface

While Francis I remained on the throne of France, Pierre Attaingnant (d. 1552) continued to enjoy a protected monopoly of the music printing business. Attaingnant had worked under this monopoly virtually since 1528, when he became the first person to begin printing music in France. However, under the reign of Henry II (from 1547 until 1559), and particularly near the time of Attaingnant's death, a variety of competitors in the music publishing business sought and received protection: among them were Nicolas du Chemin, in 1548; Robert Granjon, in 1550; Le Roy and Ballard, in 1551; and Michel Fezandat and Guillaume Morlaye, both in 1552. Because the title "imprimeur du roy" fell to Le Roy and Ballard, that firm became the true successor to Attaingnant in Paris.

However, the house of du Chemin (located on the left bank near the University, on the rue St. Jean de Latran) made significant contributions to the dissemination of printed music and books on music over the course of its publishing history, between the years 1549 and 1576. In addition to being a music printer, du Chemin was also a bookseller, a *libraire juré*, who occupied a privileged position near the University. The rue St. Jean de Latran, although changed, still exists today, and more than one bookseller is located there.

During the early 1550s, Nicolas du Chemin conceived a major project in the field of sacred music. He sought to bring certain Masses, motets, and Magnificats together into one collection, the parts of which would also be issued separately. Du Chemin's list of works to be contained in the collection (see Document III) indicates that the publication was to include seven Masses by various composers, five Masses with two motets by Cléreau, eleven festival motets (the *Moduli undecim festorum*), and eight Magnificats. Although it is not clear whether the entire collection was ever published as a whole, we do know that various parts (e.g., the *Moduli undecim festorum*) were issued separately in 1553 and 1554. Du Chemin's undertaking had precedents in the series of motets and Masses published by Jacques Moderne in Lyons in 1532 and 1546, as well as in the series of thirteen books of motets issued in 1534 and 1535 by Attaingnant in Paris. Perhaps du Chemin, reacting to competition, was attempting to solidify his position in the music publishing world of Paris.[1] Although he had issued some sacred music and theoretical prose before this, his emphasis had lain chiefly with the chanson. This publication of sacred music would bring breadth to his catalog: its size alone proposed something of importance.

Facsimile reproductions of the title page, the dedication, and the table of contents for du Chemin's entire collection of Masses, motets, and Magnificats appear in the present edition as Documents I, II, and III, respectively. The title page and first folio of the motet grouping, *Moduli undecim festorum* (motets for eleven feasts), are reproduced as Plates I, II, and III. It is the separate issue of this group, the eleven motets of *Moduli undecim festorum*, that is the subject of this edition. The majority of these motets are short-form Responds, one each for eleven major feasts of the Church year, starting with Easter. (See Texts and Translations, p. xvi, for a discussion of the nature of the texts set in these motets.)

The Music

The period between the death of Josquin in 1521 and Lassus's overwhelming influence in France, signaled by the first publication of his sacred music there in 1564 (motets, *Primus liber*, Le Roy and Ballard—LRB 82; based on the earlier Antwerp edition, 1555), marked a time when common style characteristics emerged by which music could be identified as typically "French." The two major music publishing centers of Lyons and Paris turned out a large number of music books, with chansons receiving primary attention.[2]

The Composers

Six composers (all of whom were living, but none of whom were young, in 1554) are represented in *Moduli undecim festorum*. Their works are typical of composition in the age of Sermisy and Janequin. Two of these six composers brought an international flavor to the set. The other four, who provided the majority of the music for *Moduli undecim festorum*, served to root the collection firmly in the Parisian orbit.

The two non-Parisians were Nicolas Gombert (d. ca. 1560) and Antoine Gardane (d. 1569). Gombert was a Flamand who served for some fourteen years in the court of Charles V. In 1554 he was probably living in Tournai.[3] Gardane was born in France, but, having migrated to Italy while still in his 20s, he gained prominence principally as a music publisher in Venice after 1537. Du Chemin doubtless wished to pay him homage by concluding the *Moduli undecim festorum* with a piece from this distinguished colleague.

Composers in the Parisian orbit were Pierre Certon (d. 1572), Claude Goudimel (d. 1572), Jean Maillard, and Villefond. For much of his life Certon served as "maistre des enfans de la saincte chapelle de Paris" (master of the children of St. Chapelle in Paris—he is so identified in the *Cinquante Pseaulmes de David*; 1555; LRB 17).

In 1554 Goudimel was in Paris, having lived there at least five years as a student at the University. During his first year as a music publisher (1549), du Chemin published chansons by Goudimel. Goudimel became du Chemin's assistant (see below), and an agreement between du Chemin and Goudimel, signed 17 August 1555, still identified Goudimel as "estudiant en l'Université de Paris." Goudimel's work with Latin motets during this period is interesting in view of his growing involvement with the Huguenots—he considered his settings of Huguenot psalms to be "le plus doux travail de ma vie" (the sweetest work of my life), according to the dedication to the eighth book of Huguenot psalmsettings (*Huitieme Livre de Pseaulmes de David . . . 1566*, LRB 115).

We know very little about Maillard, beyond the facts that his significant corpus of work appeared in print between ca. 1538 and 1578, and that he was mentioned in the privilege granted Le Roy and Ballard in 1567 as one of the composers especially in demand. Likewise, details remain in shadow concerning "Villefond" (as his name appears on the title page of the source), or "Ville Font" (as his name appears with the music of the source). This possibly could be the Delafort whose works appear in print between ca. 1545 and 1578.

Compositional Technique

Three of the six composers represented in *Moduli undecim festorum* appear to have been students of Josquin. Ronsard, in the preface to *Livre de meslanges*, 1560 (LRB 68), calls both Maillard and Certon disciples of Josquin.[4] Likewise, Hermann Finck, writing in 1556, names Gombert as one of the great masters whom Josquin nurtured.[5] Certon's setting of "Homo quidam" (no. [IV], p. 26) reminds us of Josquin's treatment of the same text.[6] Josquin presented the Respond as a cantus firmus taken up in breves and longas by the tenor and contratenor, while the outer voices surround these with counterpoint in shorter note values. Certon adopted this same procedure (*prima pars*, mm. 2–17, with the cantus firmus in the secundus contratenor and tenor; *secunda pars*, mm. 2–16, with the cantus firmus in the contratenor and secundus contratenor). Certon's setting departs from this, however, in that following these openings, he switches to the more modern points-of-imitation style.

For the most part, however, in all eleven of these motets we are dealing with a post-Josquin style representative of the second quarter of the cinquecento. The texture is consistently imitative, with very little writing in familiar style. Points of imitation interlock in a texture of continuous flow. The harmonies are triadic, and full chords close off ten of the eleven motets. (The exception is Gombert's "Surge Petre," no. [VI], p. 45.) The voice parts are balanced and share equally in the polyphony. Rhythm and dissonance are highly controlled. Seven of the eleven motets are in the Ionian mode. Smooth melodic flow of a kind we associate with plainchant underlies much of the writing. Plainsong melodies were traditionally associated with these motet texts, and in many instances such melodies infuse the imitative patterns of the pieces. As in most sixteenth-century music, *tempus imperfectum cum diminutum* prevails in the *Moduli undecim festorum*, and there is no introduction whatsoever of triple time. Eight of the eleven motets are bipartite with emphasis on Responsory form. The remaining three are through-composed.

This emphasis on Responsory (A b C b) form is unusual. Seven out of the eight bipartite motets, or 87%, are cast in this mold ("Victimae paschali laudes" is the exception). The form is not readily found among the motets of Josquin nor, looking ahead, among those of Lassus. We find Responsory form in music in more nearly contemporary Italian and French prints, but not to as great an extent as in the motets of *Moduli undecim festorum* of 1554. For example, roughly 33% of the motets in two *partes* in Gombert's three books published by Scotto between 1539 and 1541 are in Responsory form; this form is used in 25% of such motets in the du Chemin collection of 1551 (NC 16) and in 33% of the bipartite pieces in the du Chemin collection of 1553 (NC 29). The emphasis on this form in the *Moduli undecim festorum* is, therefore, striking. Because the texts that suggested this form are arrangements of Biblical texts for the Office services (see Texts and Translations, p. xvi), we may project a particular liturgical need that these seven *Moduli undecim festorum* motets were designed to fill.

The Source

This edition of *Moduli undecim festorum* (RISM 1554[7]; NC 37) is based on the copy of the print held by the Bayerische Staatsbibliothek, Munich. The size of the book is 373 x 240 mm., larger than that of either of du Chemin's motet collections of 1551 and 1553 (NC 16 and NC 29), both of which were issued in partbooks. The type for *Moduli undecim festorum* is middle-sized ("Moyenne musicque") and of a kind employed earlier by Attaingnant and purchased, presumably, from Pierre Haultin in 1547.[7] There are twenty-four folios in all. The music follows the title page directly (see Plates I, II, and III) and continues until the end of the motet collection without further prose material. The twenty-four folios are collated into three groups of eight folios each. The folios in each group are not given page numbers, as such, in the print; however a system of signatures (letters and Roman numbers appearing at the bottom of certain folios) was used to guide the binder in arranging the sections in sequence. The collation is Ee[8]–Gg[8]. The signature Ee (on the title page) is wanting, as is Ff. The signatures form the repetitive pattern 1–5 (folios 6–8 are unsigned). Thus, for example, we find Gg, Gg ij, Gg iii, Gg iiij, Gg v, --, --, --. The fact that the Cléreau Masses (NC 33) are signed Aa[12]–Cc[12], with the Cléreau *Missa pro mortuis Cum duobus Motetis* (NC 34) D[12], suggests that these, taken together with the *Moduli undecim festorum*, form a central corpus to which a head and tail were added: the Masses, title page, and other material at the head (NC 36) and signed A[12]–G[12]; the central corpus of Cléreau's music and the *Moduli undecim festorum*—NC 33, NC 34, and NC 37—signed Aa[12]–Cc[12], D[12], and Ee[8]–Gg[8], respectively; the settings of the Magnificat as the tail—NC 30—signed A[8]–C[8].

In the forematter preceding the seven Masses (NC 36), the du Chemin print includes a poem (see Document II) by Claude Goudimel that ends with the line "Non incorrectum (crede) videbis opus" (You will see—believe me—no uncorrected work). The presence of the poem, together with its last line, establishes Goudimel's unique relationship to the project. As is clear from the 1548 contract with his first assistant, Nicolas Regnes, du Chemin was not a musician. The contract provided that Regnes would "monstrer, enseigner et apprendre à son povoir audict du Chemin ledict art de musicque . . ." (show, instruct, and teach as he is able the said du Chemin the said art of music).[8] Upon severance of his unhappy ties with Regnes, du

Chemin sought another musician-assistant. He found one, *par excellence*, in Claude Goudimel, who worked for him and with him as his music editor for four years (between 1551 and 1555). The success of the relationship and the stature that Goudimel attained in the business may be surmised from the way in which the two names are linked, side by side, on the title page of the Magnificats of 1553 (NC 30): "Ex Typographia Nicolai du Chemin, & Claudij Goudimel. . . ." As both composer and editor, Goudimel was able to assure that published results represented his intentions. Goudimel did not underplay his role—*Moduli undecim festorum* contains at least twice as many pieces by him as by any other composer.[9]

An interesting situation concerning printer-printer relationships and composer attribution surrounds the first motet of the *Moduli undecim festorum*, "Victimae paschali laudes." No composer is cited for this piece in the du Chemin print of 1554. However, Le Roy and Ballard republished this same motet, together with "Ascendo ad patrem," in the following year, 1555 (LRB 16), and again in 1565 (LRB 96), both under the name of Jean Maillard, and presumably this identifies the composer. Leaving aside the curious question as to why du Chemin omitted Maillard's name from his printing of the piece, however, the question arises concerning possible infringement on du Chemin's legal rights. Du Chemin's privilege, granted 7 November 1548 for six years, protected:

> tous livres nouveaulx en Musique (qui n'auront esté imprimez) comme Messes, Motetz, Magnificatz, Pseaulmes, Hymnes et Cantiques. . . . Avec inhibitions, et défenses à tous Libraires, Imprimeurs, et aultres: de ne les imprimer, ne iceulx exposer en vente, (sans le vouloir et consentement dudict du Chemin) jusques à six ans finis et accomplis, à commencer du jour, et datte que les livres seront achevez d'imprimer: . . .

> all new music books (which have not been printed) such as Masses, Motets, Magnificats, Psalms, Hymns and Spiritual Songs . . . Prohibiting and forbidding all book sellers, printers, and others from printing them or putting [their prints] up for sale (without the good wishes and consent of the said du Chemin) for a period of six full years to commence from the day and date upon which the books will have been printed: . . .[10]

This privilege was renewed with some changes in March 1555. Thus, if LeRoy and Ballard's publication of the motet did not involve infringement on du Chemin's rights, then either "Victimae paschali laudes" had been printed previously and hence did not qualify as "new," or du Chemin gave his consent, or Le Roy and Ballard made use of the period of time during which, it appears, du Chemin was not covered by a privilege—between November 1554 and the date of the second privilege (March 1555)—to bring out their edition.

Several of the motets of *Moduli undecim festorum* are to be found also in contemporary prints emanating, usually in partbook format, from such centers as Nuremberg, Geneva, and Venice. Relevant sources are listed in the Critical Commentary section on p. xi.

Performance Practice

In performing these motets, the tempo should be of good speed, but not so fast as to obscure the clarity of the texture. Perhaps something on the order of ♩ = 60–72 may suffice as a guide for the whole set. Tempo should be steady, without rallentandos or accelerandos. Likewise, mid-range dynamics should prevail without recourse to large crescendos or diminuendos.

Since there are no barlines in the source, one should avoid accented downbeats and strive, instead, for word-stress and rhythmic freedom. Tied notes are not to be performed as syncopations. Individual lines should be analyzed for their rhythmic implications. For example, in "Ista est speciosa," no. [VII], mm. 7–14 of the superius can be grouped in units of twos and threes quite independently of any barline.

Since, during the Renaissance, pitch was variable and generally higher than it is today, transposition is a possibility. At any rate, transposition would do no violence to any concept of pitch color. Transposition upward may be particularly in order for those motets whose clefs suggest they are set in *chiavi naturali* (i.e., "Surge Petre," no. [VI] and "Videntes stellam," no. [X]). However, downward transposition may be appropriate for the other nine motets, because their clef systems indicate that they are set in *chiavette*, or *chiavi transportati*. The downward adjustment that this may indicate would be greater than the probable upward one suggested by differing pitch standards. A comparative study of vocal ranges of the motets in the collection is enlightening in that it reveals that the highest pitches of "Surge Petre" and "Videntes stellam" are d'' and c'', respectively, while all of the other motets have superius parts that range up to f'' or g''.

As to performing forces, the narrowness of range suggests that boys' voices were intended. There is an average over-all range of about two octaves and a fifth for all of the pieces. Boys seem to be pictured in the title woodcut of the court at Mass from the *Pri-*

mus liber viginti missarum (1532), published by Attaingnant (ATT 33, Plate VIII). In the illustration, the choir is quite small—it is composed of eight singers in all, including the leader (presumably Claudin de Sermisy). Thus, performing forces for *Moduli undecim festorum* need not be large. If women singers are used, their tone should be of the straighter quality of boys' voices. At any rate, Renaissance vocal tone was rather tight, nasal and reedy, without vibrato.[11]

Finally, the score, as given in the edition, may be amplified in two ways. The first concerns the possible use of instruments. The woodcut mentioned above depicts *a cappella* performance, and this remains an option. However, we need only to be reminded of such contemporary evidence as the title page of Gombert's *Musica quatuor vocum (vulgo Motecta nuncupator) . . . Liber primus* (Scotto, 1539–RISM [G 2977]; cf. RISM 1541⁴ and 1551²) to find indications of possible instrumental performance, in this case by viols or recorders ("lyris maioribus, ac Tibijs imparibus accomodata"—accompanied by larger lyres and pipes of unequal length). Du Chemin's shield itself, reproduced on the title page of the large collection (NC 36) of which *Moduli undecim festorum* is a part, shows singers surrounding a choir book, together with instrumental players at the sides. Instruments may substitute either wholly or in part for voice parts, or instruments may complement the vocal lines. The second means of amplifying the given score involves improvised embellishment of individual lines. An example of such embellishment is provided in the *diminuti* by (or transcribed by) Giovanni Bassano, as shown in vol. XXXIII of the Palestrina *Werke*.[12]

Editorial Practice

For this edition the parts have been collated into score from the *Moduli undecim festorum* held by the Bayerische Staatsbibliothek, Munich. Modern clefs are used, and barlines have been added in this transcription. The original clefs and part indications precede each piece in incipits. All editorial additions, with the exception of the title for each motet and other items noted below, are placed within square brackets. Voice ranges have been included for each part and measure numbers, by fives, have been added. Note values have been halved throughout so that ◇ = ♩. The longas at the end of each section are indicated by notes with fermatas added editorially. Coloration (*minor color*, ♦♩, or ♦♪♪) is indicated by a broken bracket: ⌐ ¬. Ligatures are indicated by brackets ⌐─, with coloration in the ligature, where it occurs, indicated by a broken bracket as well ⌐▭¬ . Accidentals in the print are included in the staff before the note to which they apply. Since in the source these apply to a single note only, they are canceled editorially later in the measure as necessary. Editorial accidentals are placed above the note in question and apply to that one note only. Cautionary accidentals editorially supplied appear above the staff within parentheses.

The text underlay is reasonably clear in the source and is given in general as it appears there. The Latin text may also be found in the Texts and Translations section on p. xvi. Text repetition indicated in the print simply by *ij* is supplied in this edition within angled brackets ⟨ ⟩ ; other editorial additions are placed within square brackets. In matters of spelling, punctuation, hyphenation, and capitalization, this edition follows the du Chemin print. Brevograms, however, are written out. Certain spellings are left in the older forms used in the source (e.g., "Alleluya" and "Hierusalem"). However, the older use of "I" in words like "Johannes" and "Jesum" is modernized. The division of the word "Alleluya" is also left as "Al-le-luy-a." Where differences in spelling occur among the voice parts, they are generally resolved in favor of the form found in such modern sources as the *Liber usualis*. When such differences occur in the source, these tend to appear between *recto* and *verso*, each of which is usually consistent within itself. This suggests the possibility that two proofreaders corrected proof, working simultaneously.

Critical Commentary and Concordances

The original print, as Goudimel promised, is relatively free from error. The commentary below documents discrepancies between the present edition and the primary source. Only those differences not discussed in the section Editorial Practice are cited. In these citations, the number and title of the work in question, measure number, and the voice part are given. Manuscripts, prints, intabulations, other contemporary settings of the same text, and modern editions are also listed for each piece. However, variant readings are omitted, except in those cases where recourse to them is appropriate in order to clarify a particular problem.

[I] Victimae paschali laudes: In die Paschae

CONCORDANCES
Contemporary Editions
(1) 1555: *Ioannis Maillard . . . Liber primus* (Paris: Le Roy and Ballard; LRB 16)

(2) 1565: *Modulorum Ioannis Maillardi . . . Primus volumen* (Paris: Le Roy and Ballard; LRB 96)

CONTEMPORARY COMPOSERS WHO SET THE TEXT
Du Caurroy, des Prez, Palestrina, and Verdelot

[II] Ascendo ad patrem: In die Ascensionis

CONCORDANCES
Manuscripts
(1) London, British Museum, Add. 34726, *passim*, no. 32, fol. 111b. See Augustus Hughes-Hughes, *Catalogue of Manuscript Music in the British Museum* (London, 1906), I: 301

(2) Previously in Wroclaw (= old Breslau), Stadtbibliothek. See Emil Bohn, *Die musikalischen Handschriften des. XVI. und XVII. Jahrhunderts in der Stadtbibliothek zu Breslau* (Breslau, 1890), p. 12, no. 157

(3) Zwickau Ratsschulbibliothek. See Reinhard Vollhardt, *Bibliographie der Musik-werke in der Ratsschulbibliothek zu Zwickau* (Leipzig, 1893–96), p. 24, no. 77

Contemporary Editions
(1) 1551: *Primus liber . . .* (Paris: du Chemin; NC 16)

(2) 1554: *Primus liber motetorum . . .* (Geneva: Simonis à Bosco and G. Guéroult; RISM 1554[12])

(3) 1555: *Ioannis Maillard . . . Liber primus* (Paris: Le Roy and Ballard; LRB 16)

(4) 1555: *Secundus tomus Evangeliorum . . .* (Nuremberg: J. Montanus and U. Neuber; RISM 1555[10])

(5) 1556: *Sextus liber modulorum . . .* ([Geneva]: Bosco; RISM 1556[10])

(6) 1559: *Quartus liber modulorum . . .* ([Geneva]: M. Sylvius; RISM [1559][5])

(7) 1565: *Modulorum Ioannis Maillardi . . . primus volumen* (Paris: Le Roy and Ballard; LRB 96)

Intabulation
London, British Museum, Add. 31390, no. 89, fol. 108; MS, paper, about 1578. See Augustus Hughes-Hughes, *Catalogue of Manuscript Music in the British Museum* (London, 1909), III: 218

CONTEMPORARY COMPOSERS WHO SET THE TEXT
Bruck, Certon, Lheritier, Palestrina, Phinot, and an uncertain author in *Cantiones triginta selectissimae* (Nuremberg: U. Neuber, 1568; RISM 1568[7])

COMMENTARY
Mm. 75–76, bassus, texting of the *ij* conforms with both the Le Roy and Ballard prints of 1555 and 1565. Mm. 89–92, tenor, the source provides only one *ij*; the necessary additional "alleluya" is editorially inserted. Mm. 91–95, contratenor, the source provides only one *ij*; additional "alleluyas" are edi-

torially inserted. These editorial insertions in the tenor and contratenor are warranted by the polyphonic texture and by analogy with the initial statement of this passage (mm. 81ff.); further corroboration comes from the Le Roy and Ballard prints of 1555 and 1565.

[III] Si quis diligit me: In die Pentecostes

CONCORDANCES
Contemporary Editions
    (1) 1554: *Secundus liber modulorum* . . . ([Geneva]: Bosco and Guéroult; RISM 1554[13])
    (2) 1555: *Secundus tomus Evangeliorum* . . . (Nuremberg: Montanus and Neuber; RISM 1555[10])
    (3) 1556: *Sextus liber modulorum* . . . ([Geneva]: Bosco; RISM 1556[10])

CONTEMPORARY COMPOSER WHO SET THE TEXT
    Maillard

COMMENTARY
Mm. 33–34, tenor, the source has one semibreve too many:

e- um ve- ni- e- mus:

Although this error could have been corrected by halving the time value of d' from ◊ to ♩, one of the Cs has been dropped instead, by analogy with the reprints by Montanus (1555) and Bosco (1556). Mm. 60–68, bassus, the source gives only three *ij* indications; tenor (mm. 63–65), the source gives no *ij* indication; superius (mm. 65–69), the source gives a single *ij* indication: in each of these cases additional repetitions of "alleluya" are suggested here in brackets, and this is a solution that is consistent with the Montanus and Bosco prints.

[IV] Homo quidam: In die fest[o] Corp[oris] Christi

CONTEMPORARY COMPOSERS WHO SET THE TEXT
    Beutel, Braquet, Gombert, des Prez, Mouton, Palestrina, Senfl, and Willaert

COMMENTARY
Prima pars—M. 4, contratenor, note 5 sets syllable "qui-" in source; "qui-" moved to m. 5, note 4, by analogy with similar passages in superius and tenor (see also *Liber usualis*, 1856). M. 9, bassus, see entry for m. 4; "qui-" has been moved from m. 9, note 5, to m. 10, note 4. M. 34, tenor, note 3 is a; g seems to have been intended. Mm. 66–73, secundus contratenor, editorial texting of *ij* follows analogous passage in *secunda pars*, mm. 56–63.
Secunda pars—Mm. 14–18, tenor, source indicates *ij* at m. 14, but the text "panem meum," rather than "comedite panem," is editorially underlaid here by analogy with the surrounding imitation (see mm. 15–18, superius, and mm. 18–21, bassus). Mm. 44–

50, contratenor, underlay in source indicates that this passage is to be sung on the syllable "-ni," with the syllable "-a" underlaid to note 3 of m. 50; editorial adjustment of underlay made by analogy with contratenor in mm. 53–60 of *prima pars*. M. 48, note 3–m. 51, note 1, tenor, underlay in source indicates that this passage is to be sung on the syllable "-ni"; editorial adjustment of underlay made by analogy with tenor in mm. 56–61 of *prima pars*.

[V] Gabriel angelus: In die festo [Sancto] Johannis baptistae

CONCORDANCES
Modern Editions
    (1) *Claude Goudimel: Vier Festmotetten*, ed. Rudolf Häusler, Das Chorwerk, vol. 103 (Wolfenbüttel and Zürich: Möseler Verlag, 1966), pp. 1–7
    (2) *Claude Goudimel: Oeuvres complètes: Motets Latins et Magnificats*, ed. Rudolf Häusler (New York and Basel, 1969), XI: 14–21

CONTEMPORARY COMPOSERS WHO SET THE TEXT
    Crecquillon and Verdelot

COMMENTARY
Subtitle in the source reads: "In die festo D. Iohannis baptistae"; the present editor believes the "D" to be a simple misprint of the intended "S."
Prima pars—Mm. 23–27, secundus superius, source gives *ij* as text for these mm. Although the syllables change within the ligature, the underlay in the edition follows the prevailing imitation (see mm. 25–29, superius, and mm. 24–30, bassus).
Secunda pars—M. 15, superius, source gives "-gnus" on note 2; editorial adjustment, which places "-gnus" in m. 17, made by analogy with treatment of this text in other voices. M. 44, notes 3–4, tenor, the earlier statement in the *prima pars*, m. 57, reads more simply ♩ ♩. M. 52, notes 8–10, tenor, the earlier statement in the *prima pars*, m. 65, notes 3–4, reads more simply ♩ ♩.

[VI] Surge Petre: De S[ancto] Petro

CONCORDANCES
Manuscripts
    (1) Münster: University Library. Santini collection HS. 3672* (p). The reference to the manuscripts appears to be relevant. See Schmidt-Görg, *Nicolas Gombert Kapellmeister Kaiser Karls V. Leben und Werk* (Bonn: L. Röhrscheid, 1938), p. 367
    (2) Stuttgart: Landesbibliothek. Mus. Ms. 34. See A. Halm, *Katalog über die Musik-Codices des. 16. und 17. Jahrhunderts auf der Königlichen Landes-Bibliothek in Stuttgart*, 1902–1903 (*Beilage* to *Monatshefte für Musikgeschichte*, Jahrgang 34–35, 1902–1903), p. 26. Gombert: Angelus domini astitit. 4 st. This is the

second section of the motet. See also Schmidt-Görg, *Nicolas Gombert* (Bonn: L. Röhrscheid, 1938) p. 367

(3)Uppsala: Universitetsbiblioteket, 76a, fol. 63v

Contemporary Editions

(1) 1541: *Nicolai Gomberti . . . Liber secundus/ Quatuor vocum . . .* (Venice: G. Scotto; RISM[G 2987])

(2) 1542: *N. Gomberti Musici Imperatorii Motectorum . . .* (Venice: A. Gardane; RISM[G 2988])

Modern Edition

Joseph Schmidt-Görg, ed., *Nicolai Gombert: Opera Omnia* (Rome: American Institute of Musicology, 1964), VI: 87–92

Intabulations

(1) Ochsen Kun, *Tabulaturbuch auff die Lautten* (Heidelberg, 1558), fol. 211 (RISM 1558[20]); see Schmidt-Görg, *Nicolas Gombert* (Bonn: L. Röhrscheid, 1938), p. 367 (cf. pp. 357 and 360)

(2) Warschau, *Sammlung Alexander Polinski, Deutsche Orgeltabulatur aus dem Jahre 1548* (manuscript); see Schmidt-Görg, *Nicolas Gombert* (Bonn: L. Röhrscheid, 1938), p. 367

CONTEMPORARY COMPOSERS WHO SET THE TEXT

Avenarius, Gombert, Jacquet, Palestrina, and Philips

COMMENTARY

Prima pars—Mm. 2–3, contratenor, source text reads: "Et induete"; editorial texting made by analogy with the opening phrase of the other parts and by analogy with the 1541 edition (Scotto). M. 32, note 2–m.37, note 1, superius, note 2 of m. 32 is ◇· in the source (which would be transcribed ♪⌢|♪); editorial transcription and its attendant texting follows 1541 Scotto edition as well as analogous passage in contratenor (mm. 28–32). Mm. 54–57, contratenor, texting of *ij* section is by analogy with *secunda pars* (mm. 55–58), despite the ligature. Mm. 54–57, tenor, source gives: "|-ni-bus tu-|-|-|is|"; alternate text is consistent with *secunda pars* (mm. 55–58), which provides an *ij*.

Secunda pars—Mm. 6–11, tenor, source indicates *ij*, presumably repeating the "Angelus Domini" that begins the *secunda pars*; the word "astitit" is editorially added at m. 8 to complete the text at this point and by analogy with the 1541 Scotto print. M. 29, note 2–m. 31, contratenor, source has syllable "di-" underlaid to m. 29, note 2, and syllable "-cens" to m. 30, note 2–m.31; editorial insertion of "eum" and underlay of "dicens" has been done to complete the text and by analogy with the 1541 Scotto print. Mm. 34–35, contratenor, marked *ij* in source; editorial expansion of *ij*, with "eum dicens," is by analogy with mm. 29–31 and with the

1541 Scotto print, which has *ij*. Mm. 38–39, contratenor, syllable "di-" underlaid to note 2 of m. 38, and syllable "-cens" to m. 39, note 1 in source; editorial underlay made by analogy with preceding passage and with the 1541 Scotto print, which has *ij*. Mm. 49–50, contratenor, the source underlays syllable "ci-" to note 4 of m. 49; editorial underlay made by analogy with similar passage in *prima pars* (mm. 48–49) and with 1541 Scotto print.

[VII] Ista est speciosa: De Beata Maria

CONCORDANCES
Modern Editions

(1) Claude Goudimel: *Vier Festmotetten*, ed. Rudolf Häusler, Das Chorwerk, vol. 103 (Wolfenbüttel and Zürich: Möseler Verlag, 1966), pp. 8–12

(2) *Claude Goudimel: Oeuvres complètes: Motets Latins et Magnificats*, ed. Rudolf Häusler (New York and Basel, 1969), XI: 22–28

CONTEMPORARY COMPOSERS WHO SET THE TEXT

An anonymous author in *Secundus tomus biciniorum* (Wittenberg: Rhaw, 1545; RISM 1545[7]) and Lescuyr

COMMENTARY

Secunda pars—M. 40, note 1, tenor, rhythm differs from analogous section in *prima pars* (m. 48, notes 1 and 2), which reads ♪· ♪.

[VIII] Ecce ego Johannes: In die festo Omnium Sanctorum

CONTEMPORARY COMPOSER WHO SET THE TEXT
Palestrina (parody Mass)

COMMENTARY

M. 28, contratenor, note 3 is e' in source; f' seems to have been intended. M. 51, secundus tenor, note 1, edition follows source; although c' is clearly indicated in the print, an a might make better sense in view of the surrounding imitation (e.g. mm. 51–52, superius). M. 54, tenor, note 2, edition follows source; however, f might make better sense (cf. m. 44, contratenor).

[IX] Hodie nobis: In die fest[o] Nativitatis Domini

CONCORDANCES
Contemporary Editions

(1) 1555: *Quartus liber modulorum . . .* ([Geneva]: Bosco and Guéroult; RISM 1555[14])

(2) 1559: *Tertius liber modulorum . . .* ([Geneva]: M. Sylvius; RISM [1559][4])

Modern Editions

(1) Claude Goudimel: *Vier Festmotetten*, ed. Rudolf Häusler, Das Chorwerk, vol. 103 (Wolfenbüttel and Zürich: Möseler Verlag, 1966), pp. 13–18

(2) *Claude Goudimel: Oeuvres complètes: Motets Latins et Magnificats*, ed. Rudolf Häusler (New York and Basel, 1969), XI: 29–36

COMMENTARY

Secunda pars—M. 36, notes 3–4, superius, the melodic line differs from *prima pars* (mm. 53–54). M. 41, contratenor, source gives syllable "ter-" on note 7; editorial texting is by analogy with *prima pars* (m. 58). M. 47, notes 3–4, contratenor, the melodic line differs from *prima pars* (m. 65), which reads more simply ◇ .

[X] Videntes stellam: In die Epiphaniae Domini

CONCORDANCES

Contemporary Editions

(1) 1555: *Quartus liber modulorum . . .* ([Geneva]: Bosco and Guéroult; RISM 1555¹⁴), *prima pars* only

(2) 1559: *Tertius liber modulorum . . .* ([Geneva]: M. Sylvius; RISM [1559]⁴), *prima pars* only

Modern Editions

(1) Charles Bordes, ed., *Anthologie des Maîtres Religieux Primitifs, Livre des motets* (Paris, 1910), no. 102, pp. 114–20

(2) *Claude Goudimel: Vier Festmotetten*, ed. Rudolf Häusler, Das Chorwerk, vol. 103 (Wolfenbüttel and Zürich: Möseler Verlag, 1966), pp. 19–24

(3) *Claude Goudimel: Oeuvres complètes: Motets La-*

tins et Magnificats, ed. Rudolf Häusler (New York and Basel, 1969), XI: 37–46

COMMENTARY

Prima pars—Mm. 69–73, contratenor, source indicates *ij*; editorial underlay is by analogy with text in similar passage in *secunda pars* (mm. 50–53).

[XI] Suscipiens Jesum: In die festo Purific[atione] Beatae Mariae

COMMENTARY

Secunda pars—Mm. 42–43, superius, source text reads: "ple-bis tu-|ae, ple-|"; alternate texting here is suggested from *prima pars*, superius, mm. 50–51.

Acknowledgments

My thanks go to those at Isham Memorial Library, Harvard University, for making material available, and to Dr. Robert Tangeman; but I am particularly grateful to Mr. Richard French, whose guidance was of great value.

J. Heywood Alexander

Notes

1. Three modern studies are essential to our understanding of the important Parisian publishing firms of Attaingnant, du Chemin, and Le Roy and Ballard. They are cited below, and the *sigla* are used to refer to these bibliographies throughout the Preface.

ATT   Heartz, Daniel. *Pierre Attaingnant: Royal Printer of Music: A Historical Study and Bibliographic Catalogue.* Berkeley and Los Angeles: University of California Press, 1969.

NC   Lesure, François and Geneviève Thibault. "Bibliographie des éditions musicales publiées par Nicolas du Chemin (1549–1576)." *Annales Musicologiques* I (Paris: Société de musique d'autrefois, 1953): 269–373, published separately by the Society, 1953, with supplements and corrections in *Annales Musicologiques* IV (1956): 251–53, and VI (1958–63): 403–6.

LRB   Lesure, François and Geneviève Thibault. *Bibliographie des éditions d'Adrian Le Roy et Robert Ballard (1551–1598)* Paris: Société Français de musicologie, 1955.

2. Excellent background information is contained in François Lesure, "La musique religieuse française au XVIᵉ siècle," in *Musique et musiciens français du XVIᵉ siècle* (reprint, Geneva: Minkoff, 1976), pp. 9–24. See also *New Oxford History of Music*, vol. IV, *France in the Sixteenth Century (1520–1610)* (London: Oxford University Press, 1968), pp. 237–252.

3. Much valuable information is contained in Joseph Schmidt-Görg, *Nicolas Gombert Kapellmeister Kaiser Karls V. Leben und Werk* (Bonn: L. Röhrscheid, 1938). Schmidt-Görg also edited "Surge Petre" in modern edition in *Nicolai Gombert: Opera Omnia* (Rome: American Institute of Musicology, 1964), VI: 87–92. The transcription is based on the Scotto print of 1541.

4. See Oliver Strunk, *Source Readings in Music History*

(New York: W. W. Norton, 1950), p. 289. However, A. W. Ambros, *Geschichte der Musik* (Breslau: F. E. C. Leuckart, 1868), III: 328, calls Ronsard's statement unreliable.

5. Robert Eitner and R. Schlecht, "Hermann Finck über die Kunst des Singens, 1556," *Monatshefte für Musikgeschichte* Jahrg. 11, no. 6 (1879; reprint, 1960): 132.

6. See Josquin des Prez, *Werken*, ed. A. Smijers, *Motetten*, Bundel V (Amsterdam, 1925–   ), no. 28, pp. 147–51.

7. The relevant item in the French national archives (Arch. nat., Min. centr., LXXIII, 9) is quoted in NC, pp. 270–71.

8. Paris, Archives nationales, Minutier central, LXXIII, 12 (Ier octobre 1548), quoted in François Lesure, "Claude Goudimel, étudiant, correcteur et éditeur parisien," *Musica Disciplina* II (1948), fasc. 3 and 4, p. 227; article reprinted in Lesure, *Musique et musiciens français*, pp. 229–234.

9. The motets by Goudimel in *Moduli undecim festorum* have been reprinted twice in modern edition. See *Claude Goudimel: Oeuvres complètes: Motets Latins et Magnificats*, ed. Rudolf Häusler (New York and Basel: 1969), XI: 14–46; and Rudolf Häusler, ed., *Claude Goudimel: Vier Festmotetten*, Das Chorwerk, vol. 103 (Wolfenbüttel and Zürich: Möseler Verlag, 1966). The transcriptions are based on the du Chemin edition (1554). See also the valuable analysis and discussion in idem, *Satztechnik und Form in Claude Goudimels lateinischen Vokalwerken* (Bern and Stuttgart: Paul Haupt, 1968; publ. of Schweizerische Musikforshenden Gesellschaft), XVI: 68ff.

10. Quoted in Lesure and Thibault, "Bibliographie," NC, p. 271.

11. See Thurston Dart, *The Interpretation of Music* (New York and Evanston: Harper & Row, 1963), p. 50.

12. Palestrina, *Werke*, ed. Franz Xaver Haberl (Leipzig: Breitkopf und Härtel, 1907), XXXIII, nos. 5–15, pp. 45–66. *Diminuti* for the first ten of these eleven pieces (most of which are motets) come from Bassano (1591); *diminuti* for the last piece come from Giovanni Bovicelli (1594).

Texts and Translations

The Church year provides the focus for *Moduli undecim festorum*, as the liturgical texts of these motets are arranged chronologically, commencing with Easter. The chronological sequence parallels that of the sixteenth-century calendar year, which also commenced with Easter.

The *Moduli undecim festorum* begins with motets for four movable feasts—Easter, Ascension, Pentecost, and Corpus Christi. According to the "Almanach pour 17. ans," *Heures de Nostre Dame, à l'usaige de Romme* (Paris, 1550), in 1554, Easter fell on 25 March; thus, Ascension would have been on 3 May, Pentecost on 13 May, and Corpus Christi on 24 May. The dates for the following year would have become 14 April, 23 May, 2 June, and 13 June, respectively. Since the probable month of publication for the collection was November 1554 (see discussion in The Source, above), these later dates are those for which the motets of *Moduli undecim festorum* were probably first available for use.

According to designations given in the source, the concluding seven motets of this collection are appropriate for the following festivals of fixed date: Nativity of St. John the Baptist, 24 June (no. [V], "Gabriel angelus"); St. Peter and St. Paul, 29 June (no. [VI], "Surge Petre"); All Saints, 1 November (no. [VIII], "Ecce ego Johannes"); Christmas, 25 December (No. [IX], "Hodie nobis"); Epiphany, 6 January (no. [X], "Videntes stellam"); and the Purification of the Blessed Virgin Mary, 2 February (no. [XI], "Suscipiens Jesum"). The motet "Ista est speciosa," no. [VII] is linked to a festival, "De Beata Maria," whose date of celebration is not so certain; although, by virtue of the placement of "Ista est speciosa" in the chronological sequence of *Moduli undecim festorum*, this festival may have taken place sometime between 29 June and 1 November (see discussion below).

[I] Victimae paschali laudes: In die Paschae

For Easter Sunday (Sequence)

The Latin text appears in a variety of places, including the *Liber usualis*, p. 780. The translation below is based on Dom Gaspar Lefebvre, *Saint Andrew Daily Missal* (St. Paul, Minnesota, 1940), p. 335. However, because the strophe beginning "Credendum est magis" is not given in the *St. Andrew Daily Missal*—it was dropped when the Roman Missal was revised in the sixteenth century—the translation of this strophe has been added by the editor.

[Prima pars]

Victimae paschali laudes:
immolant Christiani.

Agnus redemit oves,
Christus innocens patri:
reconciliavit peccatores.

Mors, et vita duello:
conflixere mirando,
dux vitae mortuus
regnat vivus.

Dic nobis Maria
quid vidisti in via?
Sepulchrum Christi viventis,
et gloriam vidi resurgentis.

Forth to the paschal Victim, Christians, bring
Your sacrifice of praise:

The Lamb redeems the sheep;
And Christ the sinless one,
Hath to the Father sinners reconciled.

Together, death and life
In a strange conflict strove.
The Prince of life, who died,
Now lives and reigns.

What thou sawest, Mary, say,
As thou wentest on the way.
I saw the tomb wherein the living one had lain
I saw His glory as He rose again;

Angelicos testes,
sudarium, et vestes.
Surrexit Christus spes nostra:
praecedet vos in Galileam.

Credendum est magis soli Mariae veraci:
quam Judeorum turbae fallaci.

Scimus Christum surrexisse:
a mortuis vere,
tu nobis victor Rex,
miserere.

Alleluya.

Napkin and linen clothes,
and angels twain:
Yea, Christ is risen, [our] hope, and He
Will go before you into Galilee.

More believable is Mary alone speaking the truth
than the treacherous uproar of the Jews.

We know that Christ indeed has risen
from the grave:
Hail, thou King of Victory,
Have mercy, Lord, and save.

Alleluia.

[II] Ascendo ad patrem: In die Ascensionis

For the Ascension of our Lord
   The text is based on John 16:7 and 20:17. See *Liber usualis*, pp. 845 and 850, and *Breviarum Romanum* (Boston, 1941–42), *pars verna*, pp. 725 and 729. The English translation is based on the Revised Standard Version.

Ascendo ad patrem meum, et patrem vestrum.
Alleluya.
Deum meum, et Deum vestrum.
Alleluya.
Nisi ego abiero, paracletus non veniet,
et dum assumptus fuero,
mittam vobis eum.
Alleluya.

I am ascending to my Father and your Father.
Alleluia.
To my God and your God.
Alleluia.
Unless I go away, the Counselor will not come,
and while I am on high
I will send him to you.
Alleluia.

[III] Si quis diligit me: In die Pentecostes

For Pentecost
   The text is based on John 14:23. See *Liber usualis*, pp. 889–90. The English translation is based on the Revised Standard Version.

Si quis diligit me, sermonem meum servabit:
et pater meus diliget eum,
et ad eum veniemus:
et mansionem apud eum faciemus.
Alleluya.

If a man loves me, he will keep my word,
and my Father will love him,
and we will come to him
and make our home with him.
Alleluia.

[IV] Homo quidam: In die fest[o] Corp[oris] Christi

For Corpus Christi
   The text is based on Luke 14:16–17 and Proverbs 9:5. See *Liber usualis*, pp. 1856–57, and *Breviarium Romanum*, *pars aestiva*, p. 391. The English translation is based on the Revised Standard Version.

[Prima pars]

Homo quidam fecit coenam magnam,
et misit servum suum
hora coenae dicere invitatis,
ut venirent.
Quia parata sunt omnia.
Alleluya.

A man once gave a great banquet;
and at the time for the banquet
he sent his servant to say to those
who had been invited,
"Come; for all is now ready."
Alleluia.

Venite, comedite panem meum
et bibite vinum,
quod miscui vobis.
Quia parata sunt omnia.
Alleluya.

"Come, eat of my bread
and drink of the wine
I have mixed for you.
Come; for all is now ready."
Alleluia.

[V] Gabriel angelus: In die festo [Sancto] Johannis baptistae

For the Nativity of St. John the Baptist
   The text is freely based on Luke 1:13–15. See *Breviarium Romanum, pars aestiva*, p. 773. The English translation is based on the Revised Standard Version.

[Prima pars]

Gabriel angelus apparuit Zachariae dicens:
Nascetur tibi filius:
nomen eius Johannes vocabitur:
Et multi in nativitate eius gaudebunt.

Gabriel, the angel, appeared to Zechariah saying,
There shall be born to you a son,
whose name shall be called John:
And many will rejoice at his birth.

Secunda pars

Erit enim magnus coram Domino:
vinum, et siceram non bibet.
Et multi in nativitate eius gaudebunt.

For he will be great before the Lord,
he shall drink no wine nor strong drink,
And many will rejoice at his birth.

[VI] Surge Petre: De S[ancto] Petro

For St. Peter and St. Paul
   The text is freely based on Acts 12:7–8. See *Breviarium Romanum, pars aestiva*, p. 800. The English translation is based on the Revised Standard Version.

[Prima pars]

Surge Petre,
et indue te vestimentis tuis:
accipe fortitudinem ad salvandas gentes:
Quia ceciderunt catenae
de manibus tuis.

Arise, Peter,
and put on your garments:
receive the strength for safety from the people:
You, whose chains
fell from your hands.

Secunda pars

Angelus Domini astitit,
et lumen refulsit in habitaculo carceris:
percussoque latere Petri,
excitavit eum dicens,
surge velociter:
Quia ceciderunt catenae
de manibus tuis.

An angel of the Lord appeared,
and a light shone in the prison cell;
and he struck Peter on the side
and woke him, saying,
"Get up quickly."
You, whose chains
fell from your hands.

[VII] Ista est speciosa: De Beata Maria

For the Common of Virgins and Non-virgins
   The text seems largely non-Biblical, although it is based in part on Psalm 44:5 of the Latin Vulgate. See *Antiphonale Monasticum Pro Diurnis Horis* (Tornai, 1934), pp. 679–80 and 688. See also *Liber usualis*, pp. 1209–11 and 1231–32 (cf. pp. 1256 and 1624). The text may apply to a woman saint other than the Virgin Mary. Since the idea behind *Moduli undecim festorum* was to provide motets appropriate for particular festivals, the

"Ista est speciosa" text may have become associated in Renaissance Paris with a festival honoring the Blessed Virgin Mary or another woman saint occurring sometime between 29 June and 1 November (see above). The English translation is by the present editor.

[Prima pars]

Ista est speciosa
inter filias Jerusalem,
sicut vidisti eam
plenam charitate, et dilectione:
in cubilibus,
et in hortis aromatum.

Yours is beautiful
among the daughters of Jerusalem,
just as you see her
full of grace and love:
in the marriage-beds
and in the cultivated gardens.

Secunda pars

Specie tua, et pulchritudine tua,
intende prospere procede, et regna.
In cubilibus,
et in hortis aromatum.

Stretch forth your image and your excellence,
favorably proceed and rule.
In the marriage-beds
and in the cultivated gardens.

[VIII] Ecce ego Johannes: In die festo Omnium Sanctorum

For All Saints
    The text is based on Revelation 4:1–9. See also *Breviarium Romanum, pars autumnalis*, p. 852. The English translation is based on the Revised Standard Version.

Ecce ego Johannes
vidi ostium apertum in coelo:
Et ecce sedes posita erat in eo,
et in medio sedis,
et in circuitu eius,
quatuor animalia plena oculis,
ante, et retro,
Et dabant gloriam, et honorem,
et benedictionem sedenti,
super thronum viventi:
In secula seculorum. Amen.

Lo, I, John
saw in heaven an open door:
And lo, a throne stood there,
and round the throne,
and on each side of the throne
sit four animals, full of eyes
in front and behind,
And thereby give glory, and honor,
and thanks to him
who is seated on the throne,
who lives for ever and ever. Amen.

[IX] Hodie nobis: In die fest[o] Nativitatis Domini

For Christmas
    The text appears in part in Luke 2:14. See *Breviarium Romanum, pars hiemalis*, p. 468. The English translation is based on the Revised Standard Version and completed by the present editor.

[Prima pars]

Hodie nobis c[a]elorum
Rex de virgine nasci dignatus est,
ut hominem perditum ad c[a]elestia
regna revocaret.
Gaudet excercitus angelorum:
Quia salus aeterna
humano generi apparuit.

Today for us from heaven
the King is worthily born from a Virgin,
so that from wretched man
power might be called back to heavenly things.
The chorus of angels rejoices:
Because eternal deliverance
appears brought to life in human form.

Secunda pars

Gloria in excelsis Deo.
Et in terra pax hominibus:
bonae voluntatis.

Glory to God in the highest,
and on earth peace among men
of good will.

Quia salus aeterna
humano generi apparuit.

Because eternal deliverance
appears brought to life in human form.

[X] Videntes stellam: In die Epiphaniae Domini

For Epiphany
    The text is based on Matthew 2:10–11. See *Breviarium Romanum, pars hiemalis*, p. 593 (for *prima pars*) and p. 589 (for *secunda pars*). The English translation is based on the Revised Standard Version.

[Prima pars]

Videntes stellam magi,
gavisi sunt gaudio magno:
Et intrantes domum,
invenerunt puerum
cum Maria matre ejus:
et procidentes adoraverunt eum:
Et apertis thesauris suis,
obtulerunt et munera:
Aurum, Thus, et Myrrham.

When the Magi saw the star,
they rejoiced exceedingly with great joy:
And going into the house
they saw the child
with Mary his mother,
and they fell down and worshipped him:
And they opened their treasures,
offering him gifts:
gold, frankincense, and myrrh.

Secunda pars

Regis Tharsis,
et insulae munera offerent.
Reges Arabum, et Saba,
dona adducent.
Et apertis thesauris suis,
obtulerunt ei munera:
Aurum, Thus, et Myrrham.

Kings of Tharsis
and the islands offered gifts:
Kings of Arabia and Saba
gave in addition:
And they opened their treasures,
offering him gifts:
gold, frankincense, and myrrh.

[XI] Suscipiens Jesum: In die festo Purific[atione] Beatae Mariae

For the Purification of Blessed Mary
    The text is a telescoping of the story in Luke 2:26–32. See *Liber usualis*, pp. 1355–66, and *Breviarium Romanum, pars hiemalis*, pp. 979 and 983. The English translation is based on the Revised Standard Version.

[Prima pars]

Suscipiens Jesum Simeon in ulnas suas,
exclamavit, et dixit.
Tu es vere lumen ad illuminationem gentium.
Et gloriam plebis tuae Israël.

Simeon took Jesus up in his arms,
cried aloud, and said:
"You are truly a light to lighten the gentiles
And for glory to thy people Israel."

Secunda pars

Responsum accepit Simeon a Spiritu Sancto,
non visurum se mortem,
nisi videret Christum Domini.
Et gloriam plebis tuae Israël.

It had been revealed to Simeon by the Holy Spirit
that he should not see death
before he had seen the Lord's Christ.
"And for glory to thy people Israel."

MISSAE
DVODECIM, CVM QVA-
tuor vocibus, à celeberrimis authoribus
conditæ, nùnc recèns in lucem editæ,
atq; recognitæ.

Item vndecim Moduli festorum solennium, cum quatuor & quinque vocibus: vnà cum Cantico beatæ
Mariæ virginis, (quod vulgò Magnificat inscri-
bitur) secundum octo canendi modos.

Omnia & simul, & seorsim excusa haberi possunt.

Quæ, quo ordine sint digesta & à quibus authoribus
conscripta sequens pagella docebit.

P ARISIIS,
Ex typographia Nicolai du Chemin, sub insigni Gryphonis argentei,
via ad D. Ioannem Lateranensem. 1 5 5 4.

Cum priuilegio Regis, ad sexennium.

Document I. Title page of the collection from MISSAE / DUODECIM,
CUM QUA- / tuor vocibis . . . 1554. NC 36.
Quoted from François Lesure and Geneviève Thibault, "Bibliographie des éditions musicales
publiées par Nicolas du Chemin."

Twelve Masses
for four voices
put together from the most celebrated authors,
now recently raised into light and reviewed.

Also eleven Motets of the solemn feasts, for four and five voices: together with the Canticle of the Blessed Virgin Mary (which is commonly marked as the Magnificat) according to the eight modes of singing.

They were able to have been struck off together at the same time, and separately.

What, in which order they are arranged, and from which authors (put on the list) the following little page will instruct [us].

PARIS,
From the printing presses of Nicolas du Chemin, under the sign of the silver griffin,
on the street D. Jean de Latran. 1554.
With the privilege for six years.

STVDIOSIS MVSICES LECTORIBVS
Nicolaus du Chemin, Agendicenfis.
S. P. D.

*Vantum hactenus diligentiæ, curæ, ftudij, fudoris, pecuniæ etiam collocaueri-
mus in præftátiffima artis Muficis illuftratione, nemini veftrum obfcutum effe
poteft (Lectores beneuoli) non ex ijs modo, quæ multis ante annis edita fuerát,
ceu floribus excerptis, fed ex ijs etiam, quæ recens opera noftra venerunt in lucem, Canticis, Pfalmis, Modulis, & alijs id genus. Nondum tamen tot, ac tan-
tis laboribus defatigati, fed potius iuuandæ huius rei ftudio quodammodo fla-
grátes, Miffas duodecim nunquam antea excufas, vna cum vndecim Modulis
feftorum folēnium totius anni, adiect.áq; ode beatæ virginis Mariæ vulgo Magnificat appellata, fecundum octo canendi modos, a peritijfimis Muficæ collegi-
mus, & quàm terfiffimis potuimus typis ad honorē Dei, & vfum veftrū ita ex-
cudendas curauimus, vt fimul, & feparatim pro animi fententia comparari poffint. Fruimini igitur (Lectores) nec
finatis meritò vos ἀψεύδως magno nominis veftri dedecore vocitari. Nos vero fi, quæ profecta funt á nobis, probata
effe fenferimus, conabimur (Deo fauente) Cantica, Pfalmos, Miffas, & alia eiufmodi quàm plurima breuiter
maiufculis characteribus excudenda. Valete, & boni confulite. Lutetiæ Parifiorum, 8. Idus Octobris. 1 5 5 4.*

CLAVDII GODIMELLI VESONTINI
AD LECTOREM
Carmen.

Sacra falutiferos cauffantur myftica fructus:
  Mufica concentu dulcis habenda fuo eft.
Si diuina placent, & Mufica recreat aureis,
  Multiplicis liber hic vtilitatis erit.
Nam facra funt adeo cantu exornata fonoro,
  Vt nihil auditu dulcius effe queat.
Hinc fumenda tibi, Lector, recreatio mentis:
  Hinc & habes auris gaudia mille tuæ.
His moueare bonis, vt emas hunc ære libellum.
  Non incorrectum (crede) videbis opus.

A ij

Document II. Dedication page of the collection from MISSAE / DUODECIM,
CUM QUA- / tuor vocibis . . . 1554. NC 36.
(Quoted in NC, pp. 281–282. English translation by Ford Lewis Battles.)

Nicolas du Chemin of Sens
sends greetings to studious readers
of music

How much diligence, care, study, sweat, and also money we have expended in illustrating the most excellent art of Music can be obscure to no one of you (kindly readers) not only from those things which had been published many years ago, as it were, plucked flowers, but also from those which more recently, through our effort, come to light; Canticles, Psalms, Motets, and others of that kind. We nevertheless, not yet so wearied by such great labors, but rather aflame with a certain zeal in fostering this matter, have gathered twelve Masses never before printed, together with eleven Motets of the solemn feasts of the whole year, with an added ode to the Blessed Virgin Mary, commonly called the Magnificat, according to eight modes of singing, from [persons] most skilled in music, and have, to the honor of God and for your use, so endeavored to print them with the neatest type, that they can be prepared together or separately, according to one's purpose. Therefore, Readers, enjoy [this] and do not allow yourselves to be called unmusical to the great disgrace of your name. But if we find what we have put forth approved, we shall try (with God's favor) to print in large type, Canticles, Psalms, Masses, and as many others of this sort as possible. Farewell, and take it in good part. Paris. 8 October 1554.

POEM OF CLAUDE GOUDIMEL OF BESANÇON TO THE READER.

The sacred rites produce salvation-bearing fruit:
  Music is to be considered sweet by its own harmony.
If divine things please and Music refreshes the ears,
  This will be a book of manifold usefulness.
For sacred rites are so adorned with sonorous song,
  That nothing can be sweeter to hear.
From this you are to take, O Reader, your mind's refreshment:
  From this you have a thousand joys for your ear.
Be moved by these benefits so as to buy this book with money.
  You will see (believe me) no uncorrected work.

INDEX.

Miſſa
- Salus noſtra. — P. Colin.
- L'aueuglé Dieu. — C. Ianequin.
- Regnum mundi. — P. Certon.
- Tota pulchra es. — Io. Guyon.
- Il ne ſe trouue en amytié. — C. Goudimel.
- Trop de regretz. — P. Cadeac.
- Quam pulchra es. vocibus paribus. — Iaquet.
- Cecilia virgo.
- Cantantibus organis.
- In me tranſierunt. — P. Cler'eau.
- Dum deambularet.
- Pro Mortuis cum duobus Modulis,
- Libera me. & Scio Domine.

Modul.
In die Paſchæ.	Victimæ paſchali laudes.	
In die Aſcenſionis.	Aſcendo ad patrem.	I. Maillard.
In die Penthecoſtes.	Si quis diligit me.	Ville fond.
In die feſt. Corp. Chriſti.	Homo quidam.	P. Certon.
In die feſt. D. Iohannis baptiſtæ.	Gabriel angelus.	C. Goudimel.
De S. Petro.	Surge Petre.	N. Gombert.
De Beata Maria.	Iſta eſt ſpecioſa.	C. Goudimel.
In die feſto omnium Sanctorum.	Ecce ego Iohannes.	P. Certon.
In die feſto Natiuitatis Domini.	Hodie nobis.	C. Goudimel.
In die Epiphaniæ.	Videntes ſtellam.	C. Goudimel.
In die Purific. Beatæ Mariæ.	Suſcipiens Ieſum.	A. Gardane.

Magnif.
- Primi toni. — C. Goudimel.
- Secundi toni.
- Tertij toni. — M. Guilliaud.
- Quarti toni. — P. Colin.
- Quinti toni. — C. Martin.
- Sexti toni. — P. Colin.
- Septimi toni. — P. Colin.
- Octaui toni. — C. Goudimel

FINIS.

Document III. List of all works in the collection MISSAE / DUODECIM, CUM QUA- / tuor vocibis . . . 1554. NC 36. The Goudimel Mass seems to have been printed earlier, September 1552, under the title "Il ne se treuue en amitié" (NC 26, p. 305).

MODVLI

VNDECIM FESTORVM

solénium totius anni, cum quatuor & quinque vocibus, à celeberrimis authoribus
conditi, nùnc recèns editi.

Quorum nomina sequens tabella indicabit.

In die Paschæ.	Victimæ paschali laudes.	
In die Ascensionis.	Ascendo ad patrem.	Maillard.
In die Penthecostes.	Si quis diligit me.	Villefond.
In die fest. Corp. Christi.	Homo quidam.	P. Certon.
In die fest. D. Iohannis baptistæ.	Gabriel angelus.	C. Goudimel.
De S. Petro.	Surge Petre.	N. Gombert.
De Beata Maria.	Ista est speciosa.	C. Goudimel.
In die festo omnium Sanctorum.	Ecce ego Iohannes.	P. Certon.
In die festo Natiuitatis Domini.	Hodie nobis.	C. Goudimel.
In die Epiphaniæ.	Videntes stellam.	C. Goudimel.
In die Purific. Beatæ Mariæ.	Suscipiens Iesum.	A. Gardane.

PARISIIS,

Ex typographia Nicolai du Chemin, ad intersignium Gryphonis argentei : via ad D. Ioannem Lateranensem.

Cum priuilegio Regis, ad sexennium.

1 5 5 4.

Plate I. *Moduli undecim festorum*, title page (NC 37). Source size: 373×240 mm.
(Courtesy Bayerische Staatsbibliothek, Munich)

Plate II. *Moduli undecim festorum*, first folio (NC 37). Source size: 373×240 mm.
(Courtesy Bayerische Staatsbibliothek, Munich)

Plate III. *Moduli undecim festorum*, first folio, continued (NC 37). Source size: 373×240 mm.
(Courtesy Bayerische Staatsbibliothek, Munich)

MODULI
UNDECIM FESTORUM

[I] Victimae paschali laudes

In die Paschae

8

Secunda pars

10

14

[II] Ascendo ad patrem

In die Ascensionis

I[oannis=Jean] Maillard

[III] Si quis diligit me

In die Pentecostes

Ville Font[= Villefond]

[IV] Homo quidam

In die fest[o] Corp[oris] Christi

P[ierre] Certon

[V] Gabriel angelus

In die festo [Sancto] Johannis baptistae

[Superius]

[Prima pars]

C[laude] Goudimel

Secundus superius

[Contratenor]

[Tenor]

[Bassus]

Secunda pars

42

[VI] Surge Petre

De S[ancto] Petro

N[icolas] Gombert

- tes:) Qui- a ce- ci- de- runt de __

Qui- a ce- ci- de-

- runt ca- te-

- a ce- ci- de- runt ca- te-

__ ma- ni- bus tu- is, de ma- ni- bus tu-

- runt ca- te- nae de ma- ni- bus tu- is, de ma- ni- bus

- nae de __ ma- ni- bus tu- is, de ma-

- nae de ma- ni- bus tu- is, de

- is, ⟨de ma- ni- bus tu- is.⟩

tu- is, ⟨de __ ma- ni- bus tu- is.⟩

- ni- bus tu- [is, de ma- ni- bus tu-] is.

ma- ni- bus tu- is, ⟨de ma- ni- bus tu- is.⟩

[Superius]

Secunda pars

[Contratenor]

An- ge- lus Do- mi- ni, ⟨An-

[Tenor]

An- ge- lus Do- mi- ni,

[Bassus]

An- ge- lus Do- mi-

An- ge- lus Do-

[VII] Ista est speciosa

De Beata Maria

-tum, et in hor- tis a- - - ro- - ma- tum.

- ma- tum, _____ a- - - ro- ma- tum.

et in hor- tis a- - ro- - ma- tum.

in hor- tis a- ro- - - ma- tum.

[Superius] Secunda pars

[Contratenor]

Spe-

[Tenor]

Spe- ci- e tu- a, et pul- chri- tu- di- ne tu-

[Bassus]

Spe- - ci- e tu- a,

Spe- ci- e tu- a, et

- ci- e tu- a, et pul- chri- tu- di- ne ___

- - - a,

et pul- chri- tu- di- ne tu- a, ⟨et pul- chri- tu- di-

pul- chri- tu- di- ne tu- a, Spe- ci- e tu- a,

- tu- - a, Spe- ci-

et pul- chri- tu- di- ne tu- a, Spe- ci- e tu- -

- ne tu- a,⟩ _____ Spe- ci- e tu- -

[VIII] Ecce ego Johannes

In die festo Omnium Sanctorum

P[ierre] Certon

62

[IX] Hodie nobis

In die fest[o] Nativitatis Domini

C[laude] Goudimel

68

Secunda pars

[X] Videntes stellam

In die Epiphaniae Domini

C[laude] Goudimel

76

[XI] Suscipiens Jesum

In die festo Purific[atione] Beatae Mariae

A[ntoine] Gardane

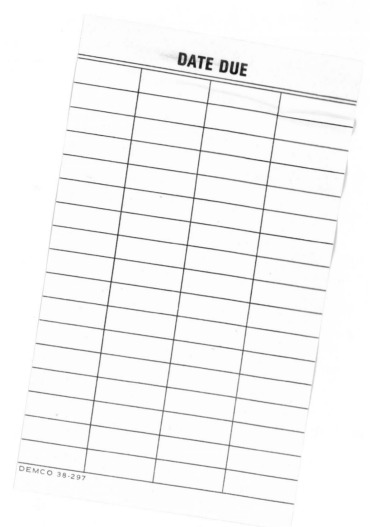

DATE DUE

DEMCO 38-297